GL🌐BAL HEROES

RISING RIVER ESCAPE

BY DAMIAN HARVEY

ILLUSTRATED BY ALEX PATERSON

MEET THE GLOBAL HEROES

MO
ANIMAL
SPECIALIST

LING
ENVIRONMENTAL
EXPERT

KEIRA
TECHNICIAN

RONAN

MATHS AND PHYSICS EXPERT

FERNANDA

TEAM MEDIC

THE GLOBAL HEROES ARE A GROUP OF CHILDREN FROM AROUND THE WORLD, RECRUITED BY THE MYSTERIOUS BILLIONAIRE, MASON ASH. FROM THE BEEHIVE, THEIR TOP SECRET ISLAND HEADQUARTERS, THEY USE THEIR SPECIAL SKILLS TO HELP PROTECT THE FUTURE OF THE EARTH AND EVERYTHING THAT LIVES ON IT.

FRANKLIN WATTS

First published in Great Britain in 2022 by Hodder and Stoughton

1 3 5 7 9 10 8 6 4 2

Text and illustration copyright © Hodder and Stoughton, Ltd. 2022

Author: Damian Harvey
Illustrator: Alex Paterson
Series Editor: Melanie Palmer
Design: Lisa Peacock

A CIP catalogue record for this book
is available from the British Library.

ISBN 978 1 4451 8297 1 (pbk)
ISBN 978 1 4451 8634 4 (ebook)

Printed and bound in Great Britain by Clays Ltd, St Ives plc

The paper and board used in this book are made from wood from responsible sources.

MIX
Paper from
responsible sources
FSC® C104740
FSC
www.fsc.org

Franklin Watts
An imprint of
Hachette Children's Group
Part of Hodder and Stoughton
Carmelite House
50 Victoria Embankment
London EC4Y 0DZ

An Hachette UK Company
www.hachette.co.uk
www.hachettechildrens.co.uk

CONTENTS

CHAPTER ONE
RAINING AGAIN

Rainwater was pouring from the roof of the Beehive, the Global Heroes' top secret headquarters. Fernanda was watching it through the window, hoping it might show signs of stopping. After a while, she let out a sigh and went to sit on the sofa. Ling was watching a television programme about rising water levels around the world.

"Can we watch something else?" Fernanda asked. "I'm fed up with all this water. I want to go out and get some fresh air."

Mo, Keira and Ronan were playing a board game at the table.

"You could take an umbrella," suggested Mo.

"I don't think that would be much help," said Keira. "Have you seen what it's like out there?"

"The valley is almost completely flooded," said Ronan. "I've never seen so much water."

"Professor Darwin says the river's burst its banks," Ling told them. "It's a good job the Beehive stands so high above the ground, or we'd be flooded too."

"That sounds like fun," said Mo. "We could swim from one room to the next."

Just then, the Beehive's alarm began to ring.

"A mission!" cried Fernanda, jumping up excitedly. "I wonder what it could be?"

"I think Professor Darwin's in the control pod," said Ronan. "We'd better head over there to find out what's going on."

The control pod was the Beehive's hi-tech hub. It was from there that all the Global Heroes' missions were coordinated.

Television screens relayed up-to-date news from around the world. Radios monitored global communications and satellite systems kept an eye on the planet's weather.

Fernanda and the rest of the team found Professor Darwin sitting in front of a huge television screen, talking to Mason Ash.

Mason was the billionaire leader of the Global Heroes, but other than that, none of them knew much about him. They didn't even know what he looked like.

"Hi, Professor. Hi, Mason," said Ronan, as they walked into the room.

"Ah! There you are," replied Mason, from the screen. "Take a seat and I'll tell you what's going on."

As usual, the man was sitting in the shadows of his office. All they could see of him was a silhouette.

"What is it, Mason?" asked Ling, sinking into a comfy chair.

"I hope it's a mission," said Fernanda.

"It is a mission, Fernanda. And you'll be happy to hear, you're one of the team that's going on it," replied Mason. "Mo, I want you to go too."

"Great!" Mo replied. "But what is the mission?"

The picture on the television screen suddenly changed. Now, they were looking at a busy street, though with all the brown muddy water flowing down it, it looked more like a river. The street was full of people, all heading in the same direction. There were men, women, and children. And all of them were carrying things in their arms or balanced on their heads.

"These people had to leave their homes in a hurry," Mason Ash explained. "As you can see, they're carrying as many of their belongings as they can."

"But why have they left their homes?" asked Ronan.

Professor Darwin explained that the street they were looking at was in Madagascar. The northwest coast of the island had recently been struck by severe flooding.

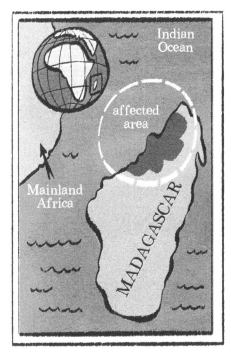

"Thousands of people have had to abandon their homes," she said. "And the water levels are still rising, so things are going to get worse before they get better."

"That's awful," said Fernanda. "Are we going to go in and help them?"

"The government are helping the people as best they can. It's animals that need our help," said Mason. "That's why I want Mo on this mission. His knowledge of animals and living things will be very useful."

"Thanks, Mason," said Mo. "I can't wait to get started."

"You'll be assisting a mobile vet," Mason told them. "That's why I want you there too, Fernanda. Your medical knowledge will be a great help."

"Lots of people have had to leave their animals behind," explained Professor Darwin. "There are thousands of farm animals, pets and even wild animals. You need to help them escape from the rising flood waters."

Mason explained that the rest of the team would be giving essential support and backup from the Beehive. Ling was to provide environmental information and Keira would follow the team's progress using the GPS tracking system. It would be Ronan's job to use his skills to monitor rising water levels and calculate the best possible escape routes.

"There's just one more thing," said Mason, as they were about to leave. "Make sure you keep your eyes open and your wits about you. You might not be alone out there."

"You mean the Evilooters?" asked Fernanda.

"Surely those criminals can't have anything to do with the flooding," said Mo.

"Perhaps not," said Mason Ash. "But as we've discovered, whenever there's an ecological disaster, the Evilooters are never far away. Remember … they are always looking for a way to make money and they don't care how much damage they do to the planet in the process."

"Well, what are you waiting for?" said Professor Darwin. "The world clock is counting. You've got 48 hours to complete your mission."

CHAPTER TWO
OVER THE FLOODPLAINS

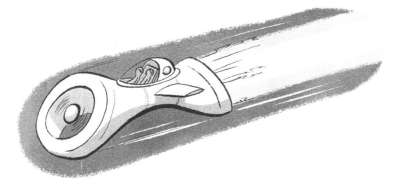

Mo and Fernanda were sat together in one of the eco-boosters – the Global Heroes' eco-friendly flying machines. Professor Darwin had already set a course that would take them towards the south-east coast of Africa, and then over to

Madagascar. They would be flying on autopilot, so all Fernanda and Mo had to do was sit back and relax.

"Good luck, both of you," said the professor over the eco-booster's radio.

"And don't forget to take your rucksacks with you everywhere you go," Keira reminded them. "The tracking chips are stitched into them. If you don't have them with you, we won't know where you are."

"I've always wanted to go to Madagascar," said Mo. "It's the only place in the world where lemurs can be found in the wild. And it's not just lemurs either, there's lots of other unique creatures and plants on the island."

"I'm sure you'll get to see plenty of lemurs while you're there," said Professor Darwin. "But it's not just exotic creatures that need your help. There will be lots of pets and farm animals too."

The professor told them that they would be landing at an animal hospital run by Dr Hanitra Rakoto. "She and her small team are working hard to get food and medical supplies to animals that need it," said the professor. "She could really use your help."

"That's great," said Mo. "We can't wait to get there can we, Fernanda?"

Fernanda didn't reply. When Mo looked round, he saw she was fast asleep.

"It's a good job we're flying on autopilot," said Mo. "Fernanda's asleep."

Keira and the others at the Beehive could be heard laughing over the eco-booster's radio.

"She always does that," said Keira. "You might as well get some sleep too.

There won't be time to rest when you get to Madagascar."

Mo looked through the cockpit of the eco-booster. Far below he could see a vast continent whizzing by beneath them. He guessed it was Africa, but he didn't know for sure.

★★★

"Mo! Mo!" said Fernanda, gently shaking Mo's arm. "Wake up! We're nearly there."

Mo opened his eyes and sat up. "Who? What? Where?" he said, peering through the eco-booster's canopy.

"Madagascar!" said Fernanda. "And just look at it. Look at all the water."

Far below them was a large town

with many of its
buildings surrounded
by water. Here and
there were patches
of dry land where
the ground was
higher, but most
of it was completely
flooded. One road
that they could see
leading out of town
ended at the edge
of huge expanse
of water.

"Look at the size of that lake," said Mo.

"That's not a lake," said Fernanda. "According to my map, that should be farmland with a couple of rivers running through it."

"There was too much water for the rivers to handle," said Ling, over the radio. "They burst their banks and created the huge floodplain that you can see."

Leaving the town behind, the floodplain stretched away into the distance. Tall trees, the occasional building, and the odd patch of raised land were the only things that showed they weren't actually flying over a lake.

"What caused all this?" asked Mo.

"A tropical cyclone," said Ling, over the radio from the Beehive.

"Is that like a hurricane?" asked Fernanda. "I remember there was a hurricane in Brazil when I was little." Mo shook his head and frowned.

"I'm confused," he said. "Was it a hurricane, a typhoon or a cyclone?"

"It does sound confusing, doesn't it," said Ling. "But they are all the same thing really." Ling explained that a cyclone was a powerful weather system.

"They form over the tropical seas where the water is warm," she told them. "The water warms the air, and the air spirals and rises quickly. When the air cools again it forms big swirling clouds that produce heavy rainfall."

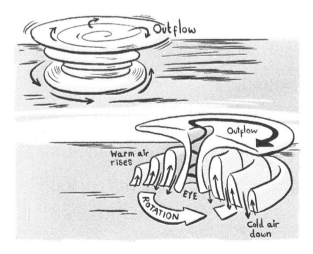

She told them that when the wind in the cyclone gets very strong, they call them typhoons or hurricanes.

"So, typhoons and hurricanes are both cyclones," said Mo.

"Yes, but the name all depends on where they are," said Ling. "In the west they are called hurricanes, but in the south, over the Pacific or Indian Ocean, they are called typhoons. When these cyclones reach land, the combination of strong winds and heavy rains can be devastating."

They flew on in silence for a few minutes, Fernanda and Mo looking in disbelief at the damage the cyclone had caused. Mo spotted a couple of cars being carried along by the current as the flood water swept across the land. Then, as they flew over a village, they saw a helicopter hovering over a small hut.

On the roof, they could see the family huddled together, waiting to be rescued. Fernanda took control of their eco-booster and hovered close by so they could watch what was happening.

"I never realised just how much trouble floods could cause," said Mo, as one of the helicopter crew began slowly lowering himself down on a winch. Once the crew member was on the roof of the hut, he fastened a harness to the mother and baby, then carefully lifted them back up.

"Perhaps we could do that with any animals that we find," suggested Mo.

"The eco-boosters are certainly

powerful enough to carry more weight," said Fernanda, "but we don't have enough room onboard for any more passengers."

After making another two trips down to the roof of the hut, the whole family had finally been airlifted to safety. The helicopter pilot gave Mo and Fernanda a wave, then flew off with the new passengers on board.

"We'd better get going too," said Fernanda. "I'm switching the eco-booster back to autopilot."

Mo nodded. "The sooner we get there, the sooner we can start with our rescue mission," he said. "I just hope that some of the animals have managed to find safe places away from all the flood water."

CHAPTER THREE
DR RAKOTO

"You're almost at Dr Rakoto's place," said Keira, over their radio. "You should be able to see it now."

"The animal hospital is on higher ground," said Ronan. "The water levels are expected to rise, but Dr Rakoto says the eco-booster will be safe in one of their buildings."

"I can see the animal hospital now," said Fernanda.

Down below them stood a modern building made from wood and glass. Behind it there was a barn and some other farm buildings. A woman in a white lab coat was standing by the barn, waving to them.

"That must be Dr Rakoto," said Mo. "She's showing us where to land."

Taking control of the eco-booster, Fernanda carefully guided it through the barn's open doors. As they touched down, the woman came over to meet them. It was then they noticed she was walking with crutches.

"Hi, Dr Rakoto," said Fernanda, clambering down from the eco-booster.

Mo grabbed their rucksacks and followed her.

"Welcome to Madagascar," said Dr Rakoto. "It's great to see you both, but I'm afraid your journey may have been wasted."

"What do you mean?" asked Mo. "Are we too late?"

"It's not that," said Dr Rakoto, showing them her bandaged leg. "It's this!"

"What happened?" asked Fernanda.

"I managed to break it while we were trying to rescue some zebu, our local cattle," said Dr Rakoto. "I wanted you to help me to get food and medicine to animals that have been stranded by the floods. But now I'm stranded here myself."

"Don't worry," said Mo. "If you can't get to the animals, we'll bring the animals to you."

"That sounds perfect," said
Dr Rakoto. "Come on, I'll show you
our hospital."

With the eco-booster safely stored
away, Fernanda and Mo followed
Dr Rakoto over to the modern building
they had seen from above. Inside, one of
the doctor's assistants was busy unpacking
boxes of medical supplies.

"Sorry about the mess," said
Dr Rakoto. "We've just had a delivery,
and there's more on the way. We're
expecting lots of animals to pass through,
so we want to be prepared."

"Do you have many animals here

right now?" asked Mo.

Dr Rakoto led them to a room that had cages against the walls.

"In here we have a few cats," said the doctor, "and next door there's a couple of dogs. We've got some sheep too, but they're in one of the other buildings."

Mo crouched down to say hello to one of the cats, but he really wanted to see something more exotic. "Have you got any lemurs?" he asked.

Dr Rakoto shook her head. "Not at the moment," she said. "And that's a bit unusual really. We would expect to have a few by now. Perhaps you'll spot some when you go out."

The doctor showed Fernanda and Mo a large map of the area. Coloured pins marked locations that Dr Rakoto and her team had already visited, but there were plenty more places that needed checking. One of them was quite close to the animal hospital.

"That looks like a good place to start," said Fernanda, pointing out a small village on the map.

"Good idea," said Dr Rakoto. "But you'll have to go on foot as our boat, the *Sirenia*, is picking up the rest of the supplies."

After putting on their rucksacks, Mo and Fernanda picked up a couple of animal carriers.

"These will be useful if we find any small animals," said Mo. "We might have to wait for the boat if we find anything bigger." Then, with a wave to Dr Rakoto, the two friends set off along the path that would take them to the village.

The village was further away than it had looked, but Fernanda and Mo managed to get most of the way without walking through the flood water. Then, as the path began to slope down, it became clear that things were about to change. The village itself was completely flooded.

"Perhaps we should have waited for the boat," said Mo.

"You're not worried about getting your feet wet are you?" laughed Fernanda.

But as they waded through the water towards the first hut, they soon realised that it wouldn't just be their feet getting wet. The water was already up to their waists. "This isn't as much fun as I thought it would be," said Mo.

"It's a good job we brought spare clothes," said Fernanda.

There were no animals in the hut, but there was a dry place to put the animal carriers.

"We can leave these here while we search the village," said Fernanda.

Just then, they heard a small voice coming from Mo's rucksack.

"It's Keira," said Mo. "Can you get my radio?"

Mo stood still while Fernanda reached into his rucksack.

"Here it is," Fernanda said, pressing the talk button. "Hi Keira, we're just starting to search a village for stranded animals."

"I've called just in time then," said Keira. "I put my new tracking device in Mo's rucksack. It should pick up any signs of life in your area."

"Thanks!" said Mo. "That will be a great help."

"Just try not to drop it in the water," chuckled Keira.

Mo felt his face getting hot. He knew exactly what Keira was talking about. It wasn't long ago that he had dropped a tracking device into the Arctic

Ocean. "That wasn't my fault," he said. "We were being chased by a polar bear."

CHAPTER FOUR
THE SEARCH

Before Mo had a chance to get Keira's tracking device from his rucksack, they heard a loud crashing sound.

"That came from inside one of the other huts," said Fernanda.

"It sounds like we won't need the tracker just yet," Mo said.

"We might need a bigger animal carrier though," said Fernanda. "Whatever made that noise sounded big."

As they waded across the street, Fernanda gave Mo a worried look.

"You don't think it could be anything dangerous, do you?" she asked.

Mo thought for a moment. "Probably not," he said. "There aren't many dangerous creatures in Madagascar. Not big ones anyway."

Then, there was another loud crash.

"It's coming from in there," said Mo, pointing at one of the huts. "I'll go and take a look."

"Be careful," warned Fernanda.

Mo walked slowly towards the hut and tried to peer in through the windows. "I think I can see something," he said. "But I'm not sure what it is …"

All of a sudden, a huge shape came crashing through the doorway. Mo let out a cry and quickly stepped to one side. As he did, a giant creature charged past him, splashing water everywhere, before coming to a halt a few metres away.

At first glance, Fernanda thought it was a cow or a bull, but with its hump and long horns, it had to be something else. "What is it?" she asked.

"It's a zebu," replied Mo. "Along with lemurs, they are one of the national creatures of Madagascar."

The zebu looked at them warily.

"It's okay," said Mo, softly. "You're safe now." Mo held out his hand and slowly walked towards the zebu. When he reached it he gently stroked the animal's head. "It must have got itself trapped in the hut," he said. "It seems all right, but we need to take it to the animal hospital where it will be safe."

"How are we going to get it back?" asked Fernanda.

"A piece of rope would be useful," replied Mo.

Fernanda took a roll of bandage out of her medical bag. "How about this?" she said.

Mo wrapped one end of the bandage around the bottom of the zebu's horns.

Then he wrapped the other end round his wrist. "This should do the trick," he said. "And I can still hold one of the animal carriers in my other hand."

"You might as well leave Keira's tracking device in your rucksack for now," said Fernanda. "We'll have our hands full, and we don't want any accidents."

There were only a few huts left to check and it didn't take long to discover that most of them were empty. It wasn't until they reached the last hut that they found any sign of life.

Fernanda came out with a cat cradled in her arms.

"It was curled up asleep on a shelf," she said.

The cat miaowed loudly as she gently put it inside one of the animal carriers.

"Well, it's not sleeping now," said Mo. "I think it wants something to eat. We'll have to remember to bring food with us next time."

By the time they were ready to head back, the water level had already risen. "It looks like we rescued these two just in time," said Fernanda. Walking back by the water's edge, Mo and Fernanda could see that the landscape had already changed. Even more of it was covered with water.

Some of the trees they had seen earlier now looked as if they were growing out of a lake.

"It's a good job we didn't find any more stranded creatures back there," said Mo. "It's hard enough with what we have."

"It will be easier with Dr Rakoto's boat," said Fernanda. "We'll be able to take more animal carriers, and we'll have somewhere safe to put them while we're searching."

"What sort of boat do you think they have?" asked Mo.

"Perhaps a speedboat like that one," Fernanda replied.

The speedboat she had spotted was quietly bobbing in the water near a couple of trees.

At the back of the boat was what looked like a pile of boxes or crates. In front of those stood two men.

"What are they doing?" asked Mo.

"I'm not sure," said Fernanda. "Try my binoculars."

Fernanda turned round and let Mo reach into her rucksack. Taking the binoculars, he held them up to his eyes and focused them on the two men. "There's a lemur in one of the trees," cried Mo. "It looks like they're rescuing it."

"It must have got stranded when the floods came," said Fernanda. "Dr Rakoto will be happy to see it

arrive at the animal hospital."

The two friends watched as the men took the lemur out of the tree and put into a box.

"Hi there!" Mo called. When the men looked round, Mo waved at them. But the men didn't wave back. Instead, one of them crouched down while the other started the boat's engine.

With a loud roar, the speedboat raced off, churning up the water as it went.

"That was strange," said Fernanda.

"Why do you think they did that?"

"I don't know," replied Mo. "And they aren't even going the right way. The animal hospital is in the other direction."

CHAPTER FiVE
THE SiRENiA

At the animal hospital, people were busy unloading supplies from the boat, the *Sirenia*. Mo and Fernanda arrived just in time to help.

"We normally have to bring everything up from the river," said Dr Rakoto. "But the flooding means we could bring the *Sirenia* closer."

While they worked, Fernanda told the doctor about the men they had seen.

"They sound like poachers," said Dr Rakoto. "They catch wild animals and sell them."

"We should have known," said Mo.

"We've met people doing that before," explained Fernanda. "But we didn't expect it to happen in Madagascar at a time like this."

Dr Rakoto told them it was illegal to hunt lemurs. In Madagascar, it was also illegal to own a lemur as a pet. "But that doesn't stop people hunting them," she said. "Sometimes for food, and sometimes to sell."

"But why does it happen more when there's been a natural disaster?" asked Mo. "A lot of Malagasy people are very poor," said Dr Rakoto.  "They struggle to keep their families fed."

She explained that floods stop people earning a living the way they normally do. When farms are flooded and crops are ruined, people look for other ways to make a living.

"And one way is to capture lemurs and other creatures," said Fernanda.

"That's right," said Dr Rakoto. "It sounds terrible, but it is easy to understand why some poor farmers would do this."

Fernanda understood what Dr Rakoto meant. People would be more bothered about providing for their family than having lemurs in the wild. Mo understood too, but something was bothering him. He just couldn't put his finger on what it was right now.

★★★

The *Sirenia* wasn't a cool-looking speedboat like the one they had seen earlier. But it was completely eco-friendly. The roof was made from solar panels so it didn't use fuel that would pollute the water.

"Mason Ash donated it to us a couple of years ago," Dr Rakoto told them. "Professor Darwin designed it and we named it after the large creatures that can be found in the rivers and estuaries in Madagascar."

"People often call them sea cows," explained Mo. "But Sirenia is a much better name for a boat."

"I can't wait to have a go," said
Fernanda. "How fast does it go?"
"It isn't designed for speed," said
Dr Rakoto. "We use it to ferry animals
and supplies around."

The *Sirenia* only had two seats but

there was enough room inside to carry a couple of zebus. There was also plenty of room for animal carriers and supplies of food and medicine.

"Can I drive?" asked Mo.

"I think that'll be my job," said Fernanda, with a smile. "But we call it

Sirenia

piloting, not driving."

Dr Rakoto explained that they would need to keep a lookout for any buildings where creatures may have become trapped. She said that they would also need to look out for creatures that had become trapped in trees and bushes.

"The water levels are expected to get higher," said Dr Rakoto. "So even creatures that seem to be safe for now will need help to escape."

As they were about to set off, Dr Rakoto reminded them that there were bottles of fresh water on board the boat.

"Don't drink water from anywhere else," she warned them. "Flood water

can carry diseases
that contaminate
the normal water supply.
Drinking it will make
you ill."

"Thanks, Dr Rakoto,"
said Fernanda, as she started the boat's
engine. "Hopefully, we'll be back soon
with some animals for you."

As the *Sirenia* headed out across the
water, Mo was impressed at how quiet the
boat was.

"It's not as noisy as the speedboat
those two men were in," he said. Then, all
of a sudden, it came to him. Mo realised
what had been bothering him all this time.

"Hey!" he cried. "Dr Rakoto said that the flooding meant poor farmers had to find other ways of supporting their families."

"That's right," said Fernanda. "And we can understand why."

Mo shook his head. "But the men we saw weren't poor farmers," he said. "Poor farmers don't wear camouflaged clothing and they certainly don't whizz around in big speedboats."

Fernanda and Mo looked at each other for a moment.

"That means they could be ... Evilooters!" they cried together.

"I'm going to radio the Beehive," said Mo.

"It sounds like you might be on to something," said Ronan, over the radio. "That's definitely the sort of nasty thing the Evilooters get up to."

"Ronan's right," said Ling. "But we need proof. You'll need to get photographs or some other evidence."

"We'll do our best," Mo replied. "But we need to find that boat first, and it could be anywhere. We were lucky to stumble across them earlier."

Then, Keira's voice came over the

radio. "Use the tracking device," she said. "Remember, it picks up signals from all kinds of living things."

"Of course," said Mo, switching the tracker on. "Blue triangles for animals and red triangles for humans."

"That's it," said Keira. "And the green triangles show where you are."

Just then, the tracker let out a bleeping sound. "It looks like we've picked something up already," said Mo, excitedly.

CHAPTER SIX
A FAMILIAR FACE

Fernanda looked across at the tracking device. Lots of blue triangles were coming into view at the top of the screen.

"Wow!" she said. "I wonder what

they are?"

"It looks like the signals are coming from those buildings over there," said Mo. A little way ahead of them they could see a group of large buildings standing on a grassy bank. The buildings appeared to be dry, but they were completely surrounded by water.

"It looks like a farm," said Mo. "That explains why there are so many blue triangles showing up. There's no sign of any humans though. The owners must have abandoned the place when then the floods came."

Fernanda carefully steered them through the flood water towards the farm. "I'll get us as close as I can," she said.

Once they had found a safe place to moor the *Sirenia*, Mo and Fernanda went ashore.

"It's very quiet," said Fernanda. "And there doesn't seem to be anyone around. They must have all left when they could."

"According to the tracker there's definitely something in that building," said Mo. "And whatever they are … there's a lot of them."

Together, the two friends crossed the yard. When they reached the shed door, Mo carefully opened it and peered inside.

As soon as he did, the silence was suddenly broken by loud squawking noises. "Chickens!" said Mo, quickly closing the door again. "Lots of chickens."

While the two of them went back to the *Sirenia* for more animal carriers, Fernanda radioed the Beehive to tell them what they had found.

"Good work," said Ling.

"We're going to take them all back to the animal hospital where they'll be safe," said Fernanda.

"You're going to have to be quick,"

Ling told them. "Professor Darwin is worried about your safety."

Ling explained that more heavy rain had been forecasted and that the water levels were expected to rise even further.

★★★

After taking animal carriers back to the chicken shed, Mo and Fernanda did their best to catch the chickens.

"This is harder than I expected," cried Mo. "They don't seem to want to be caught."

Then Fernanda had an idea.

"Food!" she said. "The chickens are probably hungry. That little cat we found certainly was."

Mo ran back to the *Sirenia,* hoping there would be some chicken food on board. He was in luck. He found a large bag of feed in one of the lockers. Together, Mo and Fernanda put a few sprinkles of chicken feed onto the floor.

Then they sprinkled some into the animal carriers. As soon as the chickens went into the carriers, they closed the doors behind them.

It wasn't too long before all the chickens had been rounded up and were safely on board the *Sirenia*.

"Let's get these back to Dr Rakoto's place where they'll be safe," said Fernanda.

"It looks like there's a storm coming."

In the distance they could see dark clouds gathering over the mountains.

"Hopefully, we'll get back before the rain reaches us," said Mo.

★★★

They hadn't gone far when Mo spotted something.

"Look!" he said. "Another speedboat. And look how fast it's going."

The speedboat only had one person in it, but it had a pile of crates at the back like the other one had. As it whizzed by, bouncing across the water, the noise startled the chickens. They all began clucking and flapping with fright.

Mo went to calm the birds down, but as he did, he noticed something in the water. One of the crates had fallen off the back of the speedboat. Mo grabbed a long pole with a hook on the end. As the crate drifted past he caught it with the hook and pulled it onto the *Sirenia*.

Mo could hear noises coming from inside through little holes in the top of the crate.

"Look at this," he called. But Fernanda wasn't listening. The speedboat had come to a halt and the man on-board was watching them with interest. In fact, he and Fernanda looked like they were staring at each other.

"What is it?" asked Mo.

"That man," Fernanda replied. "I'm sure I've seen him before." Fernanda took her camera from her rucksack and began taking pictures. As she did, the man began speaking into a radio.

Mo showed her the crate that he had fished out of the water. "This fell off his boat," he said. "Perhaps he wants it back."

Mo held the crate up so the man could see it. But instead of coming to get it, the man suddenly started the speedboat's engine and roared off into the distance.

"He was in a hurry," said Mo. "He didn't even wait to get his crate."

Fernanda was looking at the display on her camera. "I knew I recognised him," she said. "It's Captain Ransom, one of the Evilooters. We saw him in Brazil. I wonder what he's doing here."

"I think the answer might lie in this crate," said Mo, carefully lifting the lid and peering inside.

"I think we can guess what it is," said Fernanda. "We'd better call the others."

CHAPTER SEVEN
IN DEEP WATER

"A lemur!" said Mo. The creature climbed out of the crate and ran up Mo's arm to sit on his shoulder.

"It seems to like you," said Fernanda, taking a photograph. "I'll send it to the Beehive, along with the picture of Captain Ransom."

"We'll need more evidence than this," said Ling, over the radio. "But it's a good start."

Then they heard Ronan's voice. "I knew we'd run into that sea captain again," he said.

"I'm not surprised he's involved in capturing wild animals," said Keira. "We know he'll do anything for money."

"We also know how dangerous he can be," added Professor Darwin. "You need to be extra careful."

EVILOOTER CHARACTERS

EVILOOTER SPEEDBOAT DRIVER

DECEPTION: 96

POLLUTING LEVEL: 77

CUNNING: 78

GREED: 101

ENVIRONMENTAL THREAT: 88

"Don't worry," said Fernanda. "We will." Mo didn't say anything. He was at the front of the boat, looking at something. Fernanda went to see what it was.

"I was trying to see which way Captain Ransom went," said Mo. "He could lead us to the other Evilooters. This might be our only chance to stop them." Fernanda thought for a moment.

"You're right," she said. "Let's see what we can find out."

Mo switched on Keira's tracking device and sat next to Fernanda. As they headed across the water, spots of rain began to speckle the windscreen. Behind them, huge storm clouds were gathering.

"Hopefully, we'll keep ahead of the bad weather," said Mo. But after a few minutes, the rain was splashing down into the flood water around them. Just then, there was a beep from the tracking device.

"There's lots of blue triangles appearing on the screen," said Mo, excitedly.

"That means creatures," said Fernanda, with a grin. "Any sign of people yet?"

"No, not yet," said Mo.

As Fernanda steered the *Sirenia* between a row of giant baobab trees, Mo kept a lookout for buildings.

"There!" he said. "It looks like another farm. There's still no sign of any people though."

"That's odd," said Fernanda, as they got closer. "There's a speedboat here."

Mo looked at the tracking device's screen again and shook his head.

"Still no sign of any people," he said.

"Perhaps they all went out in another boat."

Fernanda moored the *Sirenia* next to the speedboat and they both stepped ashore.

"We need to be quick," she said. "The water is rising, and the current is getting stronger."

"According to the tracker, the animals are in that wooden building," said Mo. "There's nothing in the one with the metal roof."

★★★

Stepping inside, Fernanda and Mo knew they had come to the right place. The

building was full of cages. Mo put the
tracking device down and went for a
look round. Some cages contained lemurs.
Others held brightly coloured birds.

"Let's get them onto the *Sirenia*,"
said Mo. "Before the Evilooters get back."

Fernanda nodded and they both set to work, picking up cages and carrying them to the boat. It took a while, but eventually, the last one was safely on-board.

"I didn't think we'd make it in time," said Fernanda.

But just then, they heard a boat engine. And it sounded like it was heading in their direction.

"You spoke too soon," said Mo. "The Evilooters are coming."

"We'll never outrun them in the *Sirenia*," said Fernanda. "What are we going to do?"

"I'll radio the Beehive," said Mo.

"They can contact the police."

"Good idea," said Fernanda. "Perhaps we can hide until they get here."

Mo held the radio up to his mouth.

"Ling, we need you to call the police," he said. But before he could say another word, the radio was snatched from his hand.

"I'll take that," said a voice from behind him.

Turning round, Mo found himself face to face with Captain Ransom.

"Run!" cried Fernanda, grabbing Mo's arm.

They had only taken a few steps when they came to a sudden halt. The two Evilooters who had been in the speedboat were now walking towards them. One had picked up Mo's and Fernanda's rucksacks from the *Sirenia*.

"And look what I've found," said a woman's voice. "It was in the shed where we were keeping the animals."

The woman was wearing the same camouflaged clothes as the three men. In her hand was Keira's tracking device.

"What shall I do with it, boss?" the woman asked.

Captain Ransom smiled. "We'll keep that," he said. "Throw the rest of their gadgets into the water. They won't need them any more."

"What do you mean?" cried Mo. "What are you going to do with us?"

"We're leaving you here," said Captain Ransom. "We don't want you getting in our way."

"Thanks for loading our boat for us," said the woman."

"Hey!" cried Mo. "That's Dr Rakoto's boat."

The Evilooters laughed as they threw Mo and Fernanda's gadgets into the water. As they headed off in the boats,

Captain Ransom tossed the rucksacks back onto the shore. Fernanda ran to pick them up.

"All I have left is water and medical supplies," cried Fernanda.

"They've not even left us a radio," said Mo. "That means we can't call for help. We're really in deep water now."

"And it's getting deeper," said Fernanda. "The water level's still rising."

"We can't swim," said Mo. "The current is too strong. We'd get swept away."

"Then we're trapped!" said Fernanda. "And no one knows where we are."

CHAPTER EiGHT
HOOKED

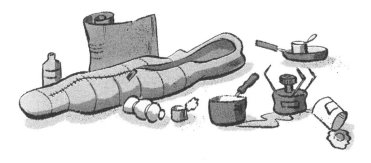

Mo and Fernanda went to see if they could find anything that could help them get away. They hadn't been in the building with the metal roof so that's where they looked first.

"The metal roof must have stopped

the tracker detecting anything," said Mo. "Captain Ransom and the woman were here all along."

In one room, they found sleeping bags. In another was a small gas cooker and some pots and pans.

"It looks like the Evilooters have been living here," said Fernanda.

"I don't think they will come back though," said Mo. "I guess they've got what they wanted."

"There must be something we can do to stop them," said Fernanda. Then Mo heard something.

"What was that?" he asked. They both stood and listened. All they could hear was the sound of the rain beating down on the metal roof above. Fernanda shook her head, but then she heard it too.

"It sounds like someone shouting," she said.

"Maybe it's the Evilooters," said Mo. Just then, the door burst open, and two figures came running in.

"Ronan!" cried Fernanda. "Keira! What are you doing here?"

"We just called in to say hi," said Ronan.

"We've come to rescue you of course," said Keira. "Professor Darwin sent us."

Ronan explained that the professor had been worried. When they discovered Evilooters were involved, she thought Mo and Fernanda might need some help.

"And we knew there'd be trouble when Captain Ransom turned up," he said.

"How did you find us?" asked Mo.

"Your rucksacks," said Keira.

"Of course," said Fernanda. "They have tracking chips sewn into them."

"Speaking of Evilooters," said Mo, "we have to stop them."

"First we need to get away from here," said Fernanda. "The Evilooters have our boat and our eco-booster is in Dr Rakoto's barn."

"You mean it was in her barn," said Keira. "We stopped to pick it up."

"Now we just need to work out how to stop the Evilooters," said Mo.

Ronan looked around the room for anything they could use. Mo pointed out some ropes he had spotted earlier, hanging from hooks on the wall.

"Perfect!" said Ronan. "We'll need the hooks too." He tied hooks to the end of two ropes. "Now we need to fasten these to the bottom of our eco-boosters," he said.

"It's like we're going fishing," said Fernanda. "

"We are," said Ronan. "Fishing for Evilooters."

★★★

The two eco-boosters were soon whizzing over the floodplains.

"Keep your eyes open for the boats," said Ronan. "We think they'll head towards the coast to meet a bigger ship."

"The police are on their way," said Ling over the eco-booster's radio. "You just need to slow the Evilooters down until they arrive."

After a few minutes, the four friends spotted the Evilooters down below.

"There they are," cried Mo.

"And there's the police," said Keira.

In the distance, they could just see the police heading towards them. It looked like the Evilooters' boats were going to get caught between them.

"There's no way they can escape

now," said Fernanda.

"I think they're going to try," said Ronan. "Look!"

One of the speedboats had come alongside the *Sirenia*. As they watched, Captain Ransom jumped across to it. Then they zoomed off.

"They've abandoned the *Sirenia*," said Keira. "Ransom is going to get away again," cried Fernanda. "Just like last time."

"Oh no he's not," said Ronan. "It's time to go fishing."

The two boats began picking up speed, bouncing across the water as they zoomed away. The speedboats were fast, but they couldn't outrun the eco-boosters. Fernanda was hot on the tail of one while Ronan chased the other.

The hook hanging from Ronan's eco-booster easily found the front of one boat, while Fernanda's hooked the back of the other. "Got it," she said, as the boat was lifted out of the water. The Evilooters inside clung on desperately. Ronan's eco-booster hovered in the air, the speedboat with Captain Ransom inside swinging gently beneath it.

Once the police boats had caught up with them, they lowered the Evilooter's boats back into the water.

"Right," said Mo. "Now we've got to take Dr Rakoto's boat back to the animal hospital."

"And then we've got to help look after all the animals," said Fernanda. "After all, that is why we came."

"I'm sorry," said Professor Darwin over the radio. "But that will have to be left to someone else. It's time for you to head back to the Beehive."

Mo and Fernanda groaned, but they knew there was nothing they could do. The mission was over.

★★★

Back at the Beehive, everyone gathered together in the control pod. Mo and

Fernanda were disappointed at having to go back so soon, but Mason Ash reassured them. "Your mission was a great success," he said. "You stopped the Evilooters, and you rescued most of the animals."

"And I got my tracking device back," said Keira, with a grin.

"But there's still so much to be done," said Fernanda.

"There's always more to be done – but it can't all be done by you," said Mason. "And that reminds me … I think I have another mission for you. And it could be your toughest yet …"

THE END

COUNTRY PROFILE:

FAST FACTS:

* It is the fourth largest island in the world

* It lies approximately 400 km off the south-east coast of Africa

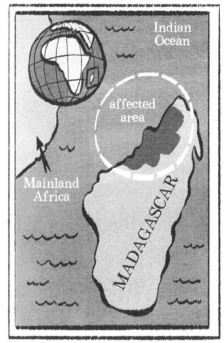

* It is surrounded by the Indian Ocean

* Most of the island is covered in grass and bamboo as well as mountains and hills

* The baobab tree is the national tree of Madagascar

* The country is also known as the "Great Red Island" for its iron-rich red soil

FACT SHEET:

Because of its unique geography, Madagascar is home to some very unusual plant and animal life. Two of the most famous creatures to inhabit the island are lemurs and zebu.

LEMURS FAST FACTS:

* They are a type of primate, have a long tail and walk on all fours like monkeys

* They mostly live in trees in rainforests

* They usually sleep in the day and are active at night

* They are mostly herbivores and eat bamboo, fruits and leaves

* Their leaders are always female

ZEBU FAST FACTS:

* Zebu are a type of cattle, like cows, with horns

* They live in herds and feed on grass, seeds and flowers

* They have a hump on their shoulders and they can use this to store food

CLIMATE CHANGE:

Human activity on Earth has resulted in more extreme weather and areas such as Madagascar are more vulnerable to flooding as a result.

CAUSE:

As the climate becomes hotter, this increases the rainfall and frequency of cyclones and tropical storms.

EFFECTS:

✱ More rain falls at once, increasing the likelihood of flooding.

FLOODING

* Cyclones and hurricanes can cause sea water to overflow onto the land in coastal regions.

* Rapid melting of snow and ice due to heat causes a surge of sea water.

* During droughts, the ground is hard and dry, so water is not as easily absorbed by the soil. A storm at the end of a dry spell can make things worse, washing away topsoil and flooding crops.

* Many people lose their homes and essential buildings in floods, and wildlife also lose their habitats.

The world is getting warmer and weather more extreme because of human activity.

It's not too late to help look after the planet.

Little steps can make a big difference …

Join the Global Heroes in their mission to protect Earth's future. Here are some ideas, but there are plenty more!

CLIMATE ACTION

1) Reuse and recycle as much as you can to help reduce waste

2) Try making shorter journeys by foot, bike or scooter instead of by car

3) Keep electronic devices and lights turned off when not using them to reduce the energy you use

4) Join a tree-planting initiative in your local community

5) Use cold spin cycles or eco settings on washing machines

6) Join a conservation team or sponsor an endangered animal

QUIZ

1) Which system is used to watch the planet's weather?

2) Which animal does Mo help rescue with a bandage?

3) Where does Dr Rakoto work?

4) Which animal does Fernanda find?

5) Which Evilooter do the team come across for a second time?

6) What are in the pile of crates on the speedboat?

7) What device helps to catch the Evilooters?

Sirenia

GLOSSARY

AUTOPILOT – a computer that steers a vehicle, such as a plane

COCKPIT – where the pilot sits in an aircraft

CURRENT – the movement of seawater

CYCLONE – a circular storm that forms over warm oceans, scientific name for hurricane

ESTUARIES – areas where freshwater rivers or streams meet the ocean

FLOOD PLAIN – low lying, flat areas of land next to rivers or streams

GOVERNMENT – people elected to be in charge of a country

HURRICANE – a large storm, often with very strong winds

MALAGSAY – name for people who live in Madagascar

POACHERS – people who catch and steal or kill wild animals

POLLUTE – to make something harmful or dangerous

SOLAR PANEL – a material designed to absorb the sun's rays to use as energy

TYPHOON – a tropical storm that forms over oceans

WEATHER – the state of the air and atmosphere

VALLEY – a low area of land, often between hills or mountains

BUSHFIRE RESCUE

JOIN MO, FERNANDA, KEIRA, RONAN AND LING ON THEIR FIRST MISSION TO AUSTRALIA

JOIN THE GLOBAL HEROES TEAM IN THESE FANTASTIC ADVENTURES:

9781445180953

9781445182988

9781445182964

9781445182971